Clifford THE BIG RED DOG®

Deck the Halls

by Maria S. Barbo
Illustrated by Robbin Cuddy

Based on the Scholastic book series
"Clifford The Big Red Dog"
by Norman Bridwell

ISBN-13: 978-0-545-03665-8
ISBN-10: 0-545-03665-8
Designed by Michael Massen

12 11 10 9 8 7 6 5   10 11 12 13 14/0

Printed in the U.S.A.   40
First printing, November 2007

SCHOLASTIC INC.

New York   Toronto   London   Auckland   Sydney
Mexico City   New Delhi   Hong Kong   Buenos Aires

It was the week before Christmas.

Emily Elizabeth and her friends had a big job.

They had to pick a tree for the town square.

"I can't wait to go caroling," said Jetta.

"And drink hot chocolate," Vaz added.

"Jingle bells! Jingle bells!" all the kids sang.

T-Bone howled.

"*Ruf-ruf-ruf. Ruf-ruf-ruf.*

Ruf-ruf-RAUUUF!"

T-Bone wanted to go caroling, too.

Cleo barked at a tree.

"That's a cute tree, Cleo," said Vaz.

"But it's a little stubby."

Then Mac raced in circles around a tree.

"That's a great tree," said Jetta.

"But it's kind of crooked."

"Clifford found a tree!" called Emily Elizabeth.

Clifford wagged his tail.

His tail hit a tree trunk.

WHOOSH!

A big pile of snow fell on T-Bone.

"Ruf-ruf-raaaaauuuuuf!" T-Bone cried.

"T-Bone, please stop howling," said Charley.

T-Bone was sad.

Nobody liked to hear him sing.

"I'll show them," T-Bone said.

He would find the best Christmas tree ever!

T-Bone sniffed at a small tree.

A star might break this one, he thought.

Then T-Bone spotted a pretty green tree.
But that tree already had a home.

All of a sudden, T-Bone looked up.

"Where is everybody?" he asked.

He could not even see Clifford!

Uh-oh! T-Bone was lost!

Then T-Bone started to sing.

"Ruf-ruf-ruf! Ruf-ruf-ruf!"

Singing made him feel better.

T-Bone heard shouting.

"I hear howling!"

"This way!"

"*Woof!*"

T-Bone's friends came crashing through the trees.

Charley hugged T-Bone.

"I'm sorry," said Charley.

"I'm glad you kept singing."

"Hey," Jetta called. "T-Bone found the perfect Christmas tree!"

T-Bone howled.

He was happy.

That night, Clifford and his
friends went caroling.

The kids sang "Jingle Bells" and
"Deck the Halls."

Mac and Cleo barked.

Clifford rang a big bell.

And T-Bone howled.

Mr. Kibble gave them candy canes.

Mrs. Diller gave them chocolate bells.

Kids came outside to listen.

And everyone followed Clifford to the

town square.

The people of Bridwell Island made a big
circle around their Christmas tree.

The crowd shouted, "Ten! Nine! Eight!
Seven! Six! Five! Four! Three! Two! One!"
The mayor flipped on the tree lights.

Clifford put a big gold star on top of the tree.

Emily Elizabeth hugged Clifford.

"You're a star!" she said.

But Clifford knew T-Bone was the real star.

And so did Charley.

"Ruf-ruf-ruf-RAUUUUF!"

Do You Remember?

Circle the right answer.

1. Why was T-Bone sad?

    a. He stubbed his paw on a tree.

    b. Nobody liked his singing.

    c. He found a crooked tree.

2. What did Clifford put on the Christmas tree?

    a. A bell

    b. Candy canes

    c. A big gold star

Which happened first?

Which happened next?

Which happened last?

Write a 1, 2, or 3 in the space after each sentence.

T-Bone got lost. _____

Emily Elizabeth and her friends went to the town square. _____

Clifford found a Christmas tree. _____

Answers:

1. b

2. c

T-Bone got lost. (2)

Emily Elizabeth and her friends went to the town square. (3)

Clifford found a Christmas tree. (1)